It's five years since Ben Tennyson last transformed into aliens and fought crime with his cousin Gwen and their Grandpa Max.

Now 15 years old, Ben is once again forced to turn to the Omnitrix to help fight a new and more sinister threat – the HighBreed, DNAliens and the Forever Knights, who team up to take over the world.

The watch-like Omnitrix has re-programmed itself and has a complete set of ten, brand new alien choices for Ben to get to grips with. Helped by his cousin Gwen with her magical powers and Ben's former enemy, Kevin E. Levin, Ben is soon all set to go hero once again!

NOW READ ON . . .

EGMONT
We bring stories to life

This edition first published in Great Britain 2010
by Egmont UK Limited
239 Kensington High Street
London W8 6SA

Adapted by Barry Hutchison

1 3 5 7 9 10 8 6 4 2

Printed and bound in Great Britain

BEN 10 ALIEN FORCE™

GOOD COPY, BAD COPY

CHAPTER ONE

DOUBLE TROUBLE

CLANK. CLANK. CLANK.

Running in armour wasn't easy, but the Forever Knights were trying their best. They barged into each other, tripping and stumbling as they hurried across a heavy wooden drawbridge which hung above a moat of churning lava.

Behind them, the thing chasing them drew steadily closer.

Into their castle they scurried, shouting, screaming for the drawbridge to be raised. With a grinding of gears and a clatter of chains, the solid oak bridge was quickly pulled up into position, blocking the huge doorway and preventing the evil monster outside from getting inside.

BOOM!

Something powerful slammed hard against the wood.

BOOOM!

The Forever Knights huddled together closely, all drawing their swords and saying their prayers.

BOOOOOM!

The drawbridge and part of the wall exploded inwards, showering the knights with splinters of wood and fragments of stone. Someone near the front of the group wailed with terror as he finally caught sight of the creature that had chased them here.

The whole castle shook as Humungousaur pushed his way into the entrance hallway. He had grown so large that he had to duck to avoid hitting his head on the ceiling. Knights fell before him like skittles as he rushed forwards, flicking his thick tail from side to side.

Across the room, one knight caught the dino-alien's eye. He was running away at speed, making his way towards another exit at the back of the hall.

Humungousaur was on him in three huge steps. He lashed out with a hand, knocking the knight hard against a moss-covered wall. The knight's armour saved him from being too badly injured, but the blow still hurt. A lot. With a groan, he dropped to his knees.

A hand that was almost the same size as he was caught him around the waist and lifted him into the air. The knight felt another jolt shake his body as he was slammed against the wall again. This time, though, he was held firmly in place.

'Answer me,' demanded Humungousaur, growling even more savagely than he usually did. 'Where is he?'

Behind his metal visor, the knight was quaking with terror. 'Why ask what you already know?' he whimpered. 'Are you testing us?'

Humungousaur leaned in close enough for the knight to feel the heat of his breath, even through the armour. 'I test your will to live,' Humungousaur snarled angrily. 'Now, for the last time . . .'

With a sudden flash of green, the alien transformed back into human form. A very familiar boy with brown hair and green eyes stood in Humungousaur's place. The corners of his mouth curled into a wicked smirk as he said, '. . . where is Ben Tennyson?'

A green and black car prowled slowly along a deserted motorway, its headlights shining like eyes in the darkness. Behind the wheel, Kevin Levin gritted his teeth and tried to ignore the . . . weirdness happening in the passenger seat.

Gwen Tennyson sat there – but Kevin certainly had no problem with that. It was the way her eyes were glowing bright pink that made him a little uneasy. And the way that same pink energy was flowing over the surface of the crushed drink can in Gwen's hand.

'Tracking Ben like this feels really weird, Kevin,' Gwen said, her gaze not moving from the glowing can.

'Hey, it was your idea,' Kevin reminded her. 'All I know is there's a lot of alien communication traffic and Tennyson's name keeps coming up.'

'Hang on, I think I'm getting something,' said Gwen, suddenly. The can seemed to pull her hands towards the driver's side of the car. 'Quickly, make a left,' she instructed. 'There's something round that corner.'

Kevin spun the steering wheel and the back end of the car swung sharply out into the road. Pressing down on the accelerator, he powered the car up a steep slope to where a large building loomed in the late-evening gloom.

It was a castle. A castle with a hole where the door should have been.

'Wow,' muttered Gwen, as Kevin skidded the car to a halt less than a metre from the castle's moat. They stood for a moment, staring in amazement at the damage that had been inflicted on the castle.

As well as the hole in the wall, large parts of the roof had caved in. Flames spat up through the gaps, sending clouds of choking grey smoke rolling up towards the sky.

Kevin's eyes followed the smoke, until he spotted a familiar red and yellow figure flying just above the flames. It was Jet Ray, one of the alien forms stored in Ben's Omnitrix.

'Gwen! Up there!'

Gwen followed Kevin's gaze, then cupped her hands to her mouth and shouted, 'Ben! Hey!'

If Jet Ray heard her, he didn't show it. Instead he kept flying, higher and higher, until he was swallowed by the clouds.

For a long time neither of them spoke.

Surely Ben had heard Gwen shouting? Why didn't he turn back?

A low groan of pain drifted over to them from behind a pile of rubble. Gwen and Kevin darted over and peered behind the mound of rocks. There, in the centre of a giant dinosaur footprint, lay a Forever Knight. His armour was dented and scuffed, and Gwen could only imagine how bruised he must be underneath it.

'Ben 10 has shown no mercy,' the knight moaned.

'Well, what did you do?' asked Gwen, certain the knights must have done something to deserve such a beating.

'Nothing, I swear on my order,' the armoured man said. 'He's ruined three of our castles in as many days.'

Kevin and Gwen glanced at each other and shrugged.

'First I've heard of it,' said Gwen.

The knight broke out in a fit of coughing

which shook his entire body. When he was finished, he spoke again. 'They say at court that the cursed Ben 10 has even attacked a hive of DNAliens.'

'Your cousin took out a whole hive?' Kevin snorted at Gwen. 'Come on. He doesn't have the guts.'

'You mean it's not like Ben to go on a mission like that alone,' said Gwen. She chewed her lip nervously and glanced up to the clouds high above. 'Why's he keeping secrets from us?'

Ben stared down at the jumble of numbers on the page in front of him. It didn't make sense. Not one bit of it.

'You get it, Ben?' asked Julie, Ben's friend from school and one of the few people who knew his secret. They were sitting in his bedroom, studying for a science exam. Ben would have given anything to be out fighting aliens instead. At least he understood how to fight aliens.

Julie spotted Ben's blank look and skimmed over the question again. 'The kid weighs twenty-five kilograms,' she began, picking up a handful of chilli fries from a wrapper on Ben's bed and popping one into her mouth. 'Three metres per second, two metres from the edge of the merry-go-round,' she continued, chewing.

Ben quickly wiped the chilli sauce from his own hands and snatched up a pencil. 'Wait, Julie, wait. I'd better write this down.'

A movement by the door caught Julie's eye. She leaned back and looked past Ben to where Kevin and Gwen had entered.

'Congratulations, Tennyson,' Kevin said, grinning from ear to ear. 'You're finally putting the Omnitrix to maximum use. You know, clandestine butt-kicking wise.'

Ben stuffed some more fries in his mouth. 'What are you talking about?'

'Nice try,' said Gwen. 'We saw you as Jet Ray, flying away from a battle.'

Ben looked from Gwen to Kevin and back again, wondering if this was the build up to some kind of joke. 'Look, I've been studying all week for a physics test tomorrow. It's my worst subject.'

Gwen raised an eyebrow. 'Maybe you're not really studying.'

'Wait,' said Julie, cutting in. 'Considering the aliens and weird transformations and stuff Ben deals with, there could be any number of explanations for what you saw.'

'You saying you can vouch for his whereabouts?' asked Kevin.

Julie hesitated. 'No. I got here a few minutes ago,' she confessed. 'He studies, then I come over to help him review.' She glanced down at the mess of scribbles in Ben's notebook. 'Not that he's acing the reviews.'

'I'm getting better!' Ben protested.

Julie patted him on the arm. 'You're making a real effort.'

'With Grandpa Max gone, we've got to rely on each other,' said Gwen. She fixed Ben with a serious stare. 'If you've got a secret you should spill it. Now.'

Ben held one hand over his heart and stared right back at his cousin. 'I swear, I've been all about calculating the angular momentum. If I don't pass, my mum'll ground me, which means minimal hero time and zero Julie time. You do the math.' He looked down at the notebook, just as Julie had done. 'Because apparently I can't.'

'I believe him,' said Kevin, almost at once. He nodded at Ben. 'When you lie your left eye twitches. But who knows, maybe you've been blacking out and sleep-fighting.'

Gwen frowned. 'Is it possible? Is the Omnitrix making you attack your enemies in your sleep?'

Ben sighed and reached into the food wrapper. It was empty. 'If we're going to discuss this,' he mumbled, standing up, 'I need more chilli fries.'

CHAPTER TWO

FACE-TO-FACE

Across town, the door of the Burger Shack fast-food restaurant swung open with a loud creak. Diners were sat at every table, munching on burgers and chilli fries, and chatting happily. None of them even noticed the boy with the green jacket and the weird-looking watch walk up to the counter.

'You all disgust me,' snarled the boy. 'This place is despicable.'

Anyone who knew him would swear the boy was Ben Tennyson, but there was something different about him. Something not quite right.

'This miasma you call food, it's foul-smelling, oily digestive preparation, everything reeks,' he said to nobody in particular.

On the other side of the counter the

assistant looked up from the fryers and held up a paper bag. Greasy oil marks had already begun to seep through the paper.

'Yeah,' he grunted. 'Probably the onions.'

The boy who looked like Ben snatched the bag and slammed some cash down on the counter. The assistant slipped the money into the till, then turned back to the fryers.

With a look of utter disgust on his face, the boy in the green jacket tore open the bag and peered inside. The sight and smell of the chilli fries made him feel sick.

'All the same,' he muttered, 'I find myself strangely craving the entire putrid experience. It must be in the DNA.'

Shaking his head, the boy reached into the bag, pulled out one of the fries, and stomped away from the counter, just as the front door swung open once again.

'Chilli fries,' said Ben, smiling at the assistant and handing him payment. 'My favourites.'

'Careful, kid,' said the assistant. 'Those double portions catch up with you.' As if to prove his point, the man slapped his bulging belly hard.

Ben frowned. 'Excuse me?'

'Friendly advice,' said the assistant with a shrug. He handed Ben a bag. 'Take it or don't.'

Outside the Burger Shack, Gwen and Kevin were sitting in Kevin's car, waiting for Ben. Gwen raised her head from her hands as the door swung open and Ben stepped out.

'Here he comes,' said Gwen.

Over by the door, Ben let out a loud burp and shook his head angrily. 'I sicken myself,' he muttered. 'Disgusting.'

After wiping his greasy hands on his jeans, Ben turned the control dial on the Omnitrix and slammed it down. A swirl of green energy wrapped itself around him, transforming him in to the moth-like alien called Big Chill.

'What the heck?' said Kevin, watching Big Chill launch himself up towards the sky. Kevin cranked the engine of his car, kicked down on the accelerator and sped after the flying alien's ghostly blue form.

Had Kevin looked in his rear-view mirror right at that moment he'd have seen the door to the Burger Shack open and a very familiar figure step out.

Ben wiped his mouth on his sleeve, smacked his lips together and looked around the carpark for the car. Only then did he spot it roaring off into the distance.

'Guys?' Ben mumbled. He hesitated for a moment then began to run after them. 'Hey, guys! Wait for me!'

It was no use. There was no way he was catching up with the car on foot. Luckily, he had another option.

'Big Chill!' he cried, using the Omnitrix's power to transform him. With a twitch of his legs and a flap of his wings, the alien set off after the speeding car.

EEEEEEEK!

Kevin's tyres screeched as he skidded the car to a sudden stop right in front of another Forever Knight castle. He and Gwen leapt out. Lasers tore through the air around them, but for once they weren't the ones being shot at.

A Forever Knight stood on the drawbridge of the castle, pumping blast after blast up into the sky. A dark figure soared above his head, easily avoiding the bright red blasts.

And then, without making a sound, Big Chill was standing behind the shooter. 'Where is Ben Tennyson?' he hissed. 'I need to know or you will die.'

The knight spun on the spot, desperately trying to raise his gun, but before he could get off a shot, Big Chill breathed. A cloud of frosty mist swept over the knight, encasing him instantly in a block of solid ice.

An energy blast exploded against Big Chill's back, making him cry out. The alien turned to find four more Forever Knights rushing towards him, their energy lances primed and ready to fire.

'Attack!' cried the largest of the knights, barrelling into Big Chill and pushing him backwards.

The other knights surrounded the alien, preparing to fire. Before any of them could squeeze their trigger, a flying kick from Gwen sent two of them crashing into each other.

With a roar, another of the knights raised his sword, swinging it swiftly towards the side of Gwen's head. A hand that seemed to be carved from living rock caught the sword's blade and snapped it in half. With a grunt, Kevin quickly slammed his stony knee against the knight's armoured chest, knocking him to the ground.

Another knight took aim with his energy lance, its muzzle pointed directly at Kevin.

Uh-oh,' said Kevin, waiting for the strike.

KLAAANK!

A wave of pink energy ripped from Gwen's fingertips, lifting the knight off the ground and slamming him hard against the castle wall. Inside the armour, the knight gave a low moan, then quietly fell unconscious.

'Thanks, Gwen. I owe you one,' Kevin smiled, jumping to his feet.

A cold breeze hit Gwen on the back of the neck. She spun around, hands raised, in time to see Big Chill freeze the last of the knights with his ice-breath.

With the attacking knights taken care of, Big Chill turned to look at Gwen and Kevin. Gwen stepped closer, her eyes scanning the alien features of his face. Something didn't seem quite right.

'Ben?' Gwen said, softly. 'Are you feeling alright? You kind of took off without us back there. We were worried.'

'You,' spat Big Chill, springing forwards and catching Gwen by the shoulders. 'You know of Ben. Where is Ben?'

Turning back into his usual form, Kevin stepped up and pushed Big Chill back.

'I knew you'd snap eventually,' Kevin said, just as the alien let out a big belch of icy air. 'Phew,' he said, holding his nose. 'Those chilli fries sure do radiate some toxic fumes.'

'Ugh. I agree,' said Big Chill. 'Everything about this planet is vile.'

'Huh? Change back, Ben,' Gwen told him. 'Let's get you home.'

Big Chill paused for a moment, a smile playing at the corner of his lips. He adjusted the Omnitrix and a cloud of green smoke surrounded him. In a flash, he transformed back into human form.

'Yes. It is I, Ben Tennyson,' he announced, slowly. 'Now you can transport me back to my domicile. There are grave matters of a personal nature to which I, Ben 10, must attend to.'

Before Kevin had time to think of a wisecrack reply, another voice called down to them from above.

'Hey, there you are! Thanks a lot, guys,' said Big Chill, swooping in for a landing. 'You left me at the diner. You really know who your friends are . . .'

Suddenly, Big Chill noticed the boy in the

green jacket with Gwen and Kevin. He quickly transformed back into human form.

Ben stepped forward and stared hard at the stranger. It was like looking in a mirror.

'So, who's your good-looking friend, Kevin?' Ben asked.

The other Ben looked him up and down. 'So you must be Ben Tennyson? A most difficult creature to find. I must speak to you as a matter of urgency.' He bowed his head, briefly. 'Please, let me introduce myself at once. I am Albedo of the Galvan.'

'A Grey Matter, hey?' said Ben. 'You're

kinda tall for a little Galvan.'

'I am the builder of the Omnitrix,' continued Albedo, ignoring the hand Ben held out for him to shake. 'And I must have it back.

'Your days as Ben 10 are at an end.'

CHAPTER THREE

ALIEN VS ALIEN

Albedo held out his hand. 'Remove your Omnitrix and return it.'

Ben pulled his arm back and clutched the watch to his chest. 'Wait, Albedo,' he said. 'I thought this was the only Omnitrix in the universe. And anyway, a guy named Azmuth built it.'

'Azmuth is a liar.'

'But the DNAliens. The HighBreed. I'm supposed to save the world with it.'

'It is incomplete and prone to catastrophic malfunction.'

Ben gave the Omnitrix a soft tap. 'Not lately. It works pretty well for me.'

'You have great luck,' Albedo insisted, 'or by now you would have ripped a hole in the fabric of the universe.'

Gwen stepped closer to her cousin. 'He could be a HighBreed trying to trick you out of it,' she warned him.

'Maybe,' said Ben. 'Why don't you show your face?' he asked his lookalike. 'It feels a little crazy, talking to myself.'

'If only I could,' said Albedo, and Ben could hear anger in his voice. 'I am stuck in a sticky, sweaty, noisy, hungry, hairy, smelly teenage human body, constantly craving chilli fries and scratching myself in places I suspect are inappropriate.'

'Wow,' Gwen muttered, 'he really is you.'

'You see, your DNA is encoded as the default in your Omnitrix,' Albedo explained. 'Mine synchronises across space and time with yours. Unfortunately, you have become my default as well.'

Kevin began to pace around the fake Ben. 'Well, which is it?' he demanded. 'Do you want the watch to fix it or to keep the universe from falling apart?'

'Both.'

'Since you built the Omnitrix, tell me how it comes off,' said Ben.

'Yes. I trust you are versed in the practical applications of eighth-dimensional quantum gravity monopole equations?' replied Albedo. Ben watched his copy's face very closely while he spoke.

'It really does twitch when I lie,' he said.

Kevin nodded. 'Told ya.'

Ben, Gwen and Kevin stood side by side, each of them folding their arms across their chest. Albedo looked from one to the other, realising they weren't falling for his tricks.

'Very well,' he growled. 'There are other ways to disarm you.'

With a flash of blinding green light, Albedo changed into Jet Ray. Flicking out his tail he sent Kevin sprawling to the ground.

Ben moved to catch his friend, but a pair of alien feet grabbed him by his shoulders and yanked him off the ground.

Gripping Ben tightly, the Albedo Jet Ray flew higher. He was pleased with himself. Snatching Ben away had been much easier than he thought.

Suddenly, he felt the boy become much, much heavier, and they began to lose height. He looked down to find the face of an enormous dinosaur grinning back up at him.

'Humungousaur!' roared the dino-alien.

Releasing his grip, Jet Ray let Humungousaur drop down into the moat. The force of the dinosaur's landing sent water spraying higher than the castle itself.

Humungousaur bobbed his head up from below the water just as twin beams of green energy streaked down from the sky. Jet Ray swooped closer, firing blast after blast at the soaking-wet alien.

Throwing an arm up in front of his face for protection, Humungousaur dug the fingers of his other hand into the closest of the castle's stone walls. Tightening his grip, he flexed his muscles and launched himself up the wall, kicking with his feet and scrabbling with his hands until he made it all the way to the roof.

Another blast hit him in the face, spinning him around on the spot. 'That really stings!' he growled.

Breaking off a chunk of rock, Humungousaur hurled it up towards Jet Ray.

The flying alien dodged it easily. 'You are not worthy to wear the Omnitrix,' Jet Ray cried, arcing around and flying straight for the big dino-alien.

KERUUNCH!

Flying at full speed, Jet Ray slammed into Humungousaur. Already groaning beneath Humungousaur's weight, the castle roof gave way, and both aliens tumbled together into the gloomy darkness below.

Still out on the drawbridge, Gwen had been watching the battle with growing horror. 'Find something to touch,' she said, her voice shrill with panic.

Kevin frowned. 'Huh? Oh!' He reached down and picked up a fallen sword. There was barely enough metal in it to allow him to cover one arm. 'It'll have to do,' he said, and he and Gwen made their way inside the castle.

Humungousaur lay half-buried beneath what had once been the castle roof. He groaned with pain, but managed to open his eyes and shrug off most of the fallen rock. A shadow loomed over him.

'Thank you for your sacrifice,' hissed Jet Ray. His eyes began to glow green, ready to deliver the killer blast.

THWACK!

A rock bounced off Jet Ray's head.

'Ow!'

Another rock hit him, harder this time. Jet Ray turned to see Kevin take aim with a third boulder. The metal arm wasn't good for much, but it made throwing easier. Still, Kevin couldn't believe he was reduced to lobbing stones. He'd much rather be in the thick of the battle. 'What a crock,' he muttered.

Jet Ray moved to defend himself, but an enormous hand clamped down over the entire top half of his body. He tried to struggle, but his arms were pinned tightly in place.

'Give up,' boomed Humungousaur, as Jet Ray fired wildly with his eye lasers. 'I'm much better at this!'

A stray shot from Jet Ray slammed against the castle wall. Kevin looked up to see several tonnes of masonry come plummeting towards him. He couldn't tear his eyes away from the falling rocks, and it was only the sudden appearance of a pink energy shield that saved him.

Humungousaur relaxed his grip for a split-second as he watched Gwen and Kevin leap to safety, but it was all the time Jet Ray needed. Twisting hard, the red and yellow alien wriggled free, and streaked off upwards to be swallowed up by the dark night sky.

'He won't get far,' Gwen said, letting her fingertips brush against the spot on the drawbridge where Albedo had stood earlier. Her powers meant she could sense the energy given off by all living things, and Albedo was no exception.

She could follow it, like a trail. Albedo's mana energy would lead them right to him. And then they would find out his plan and they would stop it.

Once and for all.

CHAPTER FOUR

FOAM PARTY

Kevin's car prowled along another motorway, weaving through the last of the evening traffic. Gwen sat in the front passenger seat. She held a chunk of pink glowing rock in her hands, and was using it to track Albedo.

In the back, Ben leaned his head against his hand and stared glumly out of the window.

'So, evil twin, huh?' said Kevin, glancing at Ben in the rear-view mirror. 'Guess you really are a hero – people want to be you.'

'Yeah, a hero with a big physics test in the morning,' Ben sighed. 'And I'd have been home studying if you'd have listened to me in the first place.'

'But who knows what damage Albedo will be doing if we don't track him down?' replied Gwen, before a shimmer of energy shook her hands. 'Turn here!' she cried.

Kevin twisted the steering wheel, pulled up the handbrake, and slid the car sharply around the corner.

The car's engine roared as it sped along a narrow road and into the car park of a large factory. Ben, Gwen and Kevin pushed open their doors and stepped out, only to be met by dozens of screaming factory workers.

'Help! Monster!' shrieked one of the workers, as they ran past the car.

'It ate through the loading dock!' screamed another.

Ben glanced at his companions, briefly nodded his head, then they all set off for the front door of the factory.

Inside, the factory was a mess. Computer terminals lay smashed on the floor, among a tangle of broken keyboards and exposed power cables. A bead of sweat formed on Gwen's brow as she fought to keep her concentration. But it was no use. With a flicker, the glowing rock went dim and dropped to the floor.

'It's impossible. There are too many machines here and not enough living things,' Gwen grumbled. 'I can't track Albedo.'

'We'll have to split up,' Ben suggested. 'Let's see if we can surround him. We can't let him escape again.'

Gwen raised an eyebrow. 'How will we know which one's the real you?'

Kevin had already come up with a solution

to that problem. Picking up a marker pen from a nearby desk, he drew a large black cross on Ben's cheek.

'Hey!' complained Ben.

'We'll call you Ben X,' replied Kevin, grinning from ear to ear.

Spitting on to his thumb, Ben wiped the pen mark away and gave Kevin an angry glare. Then, without another word, he headed off into the depths of the factory, leaving Kevin and Gwen to set off in the opposite direction. If Albedo was in here, they'd find him.

Over by a stack of wooden crates, a glowing green sludge oozed its way between the boxes and down onto the floor. The alien Goop wriggled and squirmed as he pulled himself into his normal shape, before a bright flash of green energy transformed him back into his human form.

Gwen and Kevin crept around the huge crates to find Ben standing just a few metres ahead of them. 'Guys,' he whispered. 'Come over here, I think I've found just what we've been looking for.'

Kevin narrowed his eyes. 'Hey, didn't you go the other way? How do we know that it's really you?'

'Well, um,' the boy said, uncertainly. 'Oh, man, I should not have erased that cross you drew on my face.'

With a nod of his head, Kevin agreed. Together, he and Gwen walked between the stacks of crates to where Ben had been pointing. They didn't notice him duck behind a pile of boxes, a wicked smile stretching his lips.

'Hit the deck!' cried a voice from much further along the corridor.

Kevin and Gwen whipped around to see Ben way off in the distance, running towards them. But if Ben was back there, then that meant . . .

Albedo jumped out from behind the pile

of boxes. He was pointing a large red hose right at Kevin and Gwen. Cackling with laughter, Albedo yanked open the nozzle lever. A powerful stream of thick, gloopy foam splurted out from the hose. It hit Kevin and Gwen at the same time, coating them from their necks all the way down to their feet.

'Woah!' Kevin shouted, trying to fight against the stinky foam. 'What's going on?'

By the time the Ben imposter switched the hose off, the foam had set hard. Their heads were the only parts of Kevin and Gwen still visible, everything else was well and truly stuck beneath the rock-solid foam.

'This reeks,' groaned Kevin, struggling to free himself. 'He got us with packing foam. There's no leverage.'

Gwen tried breaking free, too, but the hardened foam gripped them both too tightly. No matter how hard they pushed, there was no way of breaking free.

'Ben!' Kevin called over. 'Get us out of this disgusting stuff!'

Ben looked at Kevin and Gwen, and then back to Albedo.

'Look, Albedo, you're never going to get my Omnitrix,' said Ben, being careful to stay out of range of the hose. 'Just let them go. You know I can kick your butt.'

'Aha, but what you haven't yet learned is that I have all of your powers, Ben Tennyson,' Albedo smirked, 'and a far superior intellect. You have no choice. You must surrender, if you value your life.'

'Oh, really? Why? Because that would be so much smarter,' sneered Ben, slowly reaching down for the Omnitrix.

SLAM!

Ben's hand came down hard on the watch, triggering another incredible transformation.

Every part of him – his skin, his hair, his bones – seemed to melt into a big puddle of glistening green, before forming into a tall, vaguely human-looking shape.

'Goop!' chirped the slimy alien, flexing his goo-like muscles.

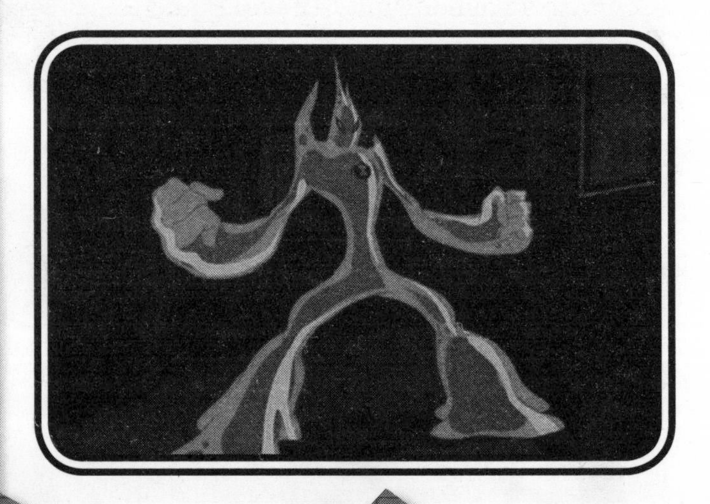

Roaring with anger, Albedo opened the nozzle of the hose and blasted a stream of stinky foam towards the alien. Goop swiftly leapt upwards, changing shape in mid-air a dozen times as he avoided Albedo's shots.

Raising a squidgy arm, Goop splattered the floor around Albedo with toxic green slime. The goo hissed noisily as it burned through the warehouse floor like acid. Albedo soon realised that packing foam was no longer going to cut it as a weapon. Luckily for him, he had a much more powerful weapon up his sleeve.

With a flash of light, Albedo struck his own Omnitrix and transformed into the towering Humungousaur. Raising a tree-trunk leg, the dinosaur alien kicked a shelving unit, sending it hurtling towards Goop. The metal shelf-edges sliced straight through the alien's gooey body. Goop dropped to the floor in many different pieces. He flopped around wildly for a few seconds, then he quickly pulled himself back together.

Looking up, Goop saw Humungousaur crashing along the corridor towards him. Hitting the Omnitrix emblem on his chest he quickly transformed once again.

'Swampfire!' he cried, leaping up to his feet and throwing himself sideways just as Humungousaur's tail smashed down on the spot where he'd just been.

'Hey, big guy! Here's some mud in your eye!' said Swampfire, hurling handfuls of his own toxic mud at the dino-alien's face. The mud burned at Humungousaur's eyes, blinding him for a few seconds.

Swampfire took full advantage and hammered him with fireballs, driving him back along the corridor.

Meanwhile, Gwen was determined not to miss another minute of the battle. Focusing all of her energy powers through her eyes, she began to shoot out pink lasers. The lasers were melting away the rigid foam surrounding her and Kevin.

'Ow!' Kevin yelped. 'Hot.'

'Sorry!' said Gwen. 'But just hold still. I am sure I can burn our way out of here! We've got to help Ben.'

Another fireball hit Humungousaur, and another, and another. Reeling, the giant alien fumbled for the Omnitrix. He activated it just as another of Swampfire's flame bolts rocketed towards him.

Just in time, Albedo switched from Humungousaur to Big Chill. Swampfire's burning fireballs passed harmlessly through him and exploded against the back wall of the factory.

Big Chill sucked air deep into his lungs. The air cooled rapidly inside his ghostly body, and when he opened his mouth again a cloud of ice cold breath blew all over Swampfire's raging flames.

The frozen air put out the alien hero's fireballs, but that wasn't all. As Big Chill continued to blow, Swampfire felt his arms and legs become stiff. He quickly tried to lift his feet, but they were frozen to the floor. He tried to move his hands, but he could no longer feel any of his fingers.

As a layer of thick frost formed over Swampfire's body, a terrible realisation struck him: he was freezing.

He was freezing to death.

CHAPTER FIVE

CONFISCATED

The cold bit at Swampfire, numbing his whole body. How long could he stand it? A few minutes? A few seconds? If he was going to survive, he had to do something – and fast.

Summoning all his strength, Swampfire forced one of his arms to move. All the while, Big Chill was firing more ice blasts.

'Must get free . . .' Swampfire slowly muttered to himself.

Swampfire tried to lift his arm again. This time freezing ice covering his arm cracked under the force of his alien muscles. He managed to reach up to the Omnitrix emblem on his chest.

The change happened quickly. Swampfire grew shorter and wider. Extra legs sprouted from his side and a hard shell began to form around him.

'Brain Storm!' he cried, shaking off the last of the ice. 'Tremble before my electrolocutive power, you feckless facsimile.'

The top of the crab-alien's shell lifted up, exposing his enormous pink brain. Yellow sparks of electricity flickered across the wobbly surface, before forming into a powerful lightning bolt. The lightning stabbed up at Big Chill, hitting him squarely on the chest.

Big Chill threw back his head and howled in pain as the electricity flowed through his body. His wings curled in around him and he fell towards the floor, but not before he slammed his hand against his Omnitrix.

It wasn't Big Chill who hit the ground, but six duplicates of the alien, Echo Echo, who had the power to make multiple copies of himself. Every one of them cried out in shock as they slammed against the floor, but they were quickly on their feet again and rushing to

surround Brain Storm.

Brain Storm shot at them with more electrical blasts, but the little aliens moved too quickly, leaping and bounding this way and that, avoiding every lightning bolt.

Exhausted, Brain Storm stopped firing for a moment. The Echo Echo clones quickly gathered together and closed in around him, a menacing look on their faces.

'Surrender. Or die. Surrender. Or die. Surrender. Or die. Surrender. Or die,' they chanted over and over again, before opening their mouths wide and unleashing six sonic blasts at the helpless Brain Storm.

'Deucedly difficult to cogitate,' Brain Storm groaned, throwing up two of his crab arms for protection. With another arm, he tapped the Omnitrix. A green flash of light shone across the warehouse and yet another transformation began.

'Jet Ray!' Ben cried, flipping up into the air and out of the paths of the sonic blasts. Flicking up his giant tail, the flying alien blasted lasers at the Echo Echoes below, sending them running for cover.

'You can't keep this up! You are too weak. You will not beat us!' they yelled up at Jet Ray, as one of them triggered his Omnitrix. In a blinding flash of light, they merged back into one and the evil imposter became the mighty Spidermonkey.

This time it was Spidermonkey's time to put his mighty tail to use. Raising it high above his head he shot thick strands of webbing up at

Jet Ray, sticking him to the ceiling.

Bouncing once on the floor, Spidermonkey leapt up to the ceiling, landing right beside the trapped Jet Ray.

'You have reached the end. Your Omnitrix will soon lose all of its power,' the eight-legged alien growled, hitting Jet Ray with a series of hard punches across the jaw.

'Yield. Yield. Yield!' he shouted, between punches. 'You cannot win.'

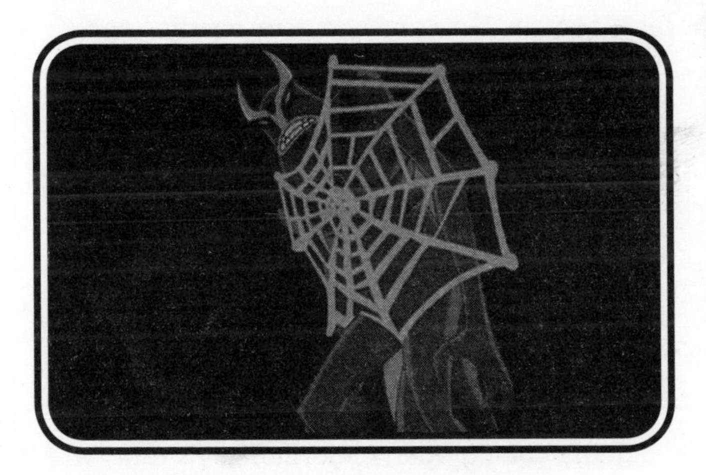

The pain was almost too much to bear, but there was no way Jet Ray was giving up that easily. A power blast from his eyes knocked Spidermonkey back down to the floor, buying him a few seconds.

Squirming around in the rock-hard steel web, Jet Ray tried to pull a hand free from the web. It wouldn't budge.

'Come on, get free!' Jet Ray muttered, using all of his might to free himself.

With one last push, Jet Ray managed to get a hand free. He quickly slammed down on the Omnitrix.

'Let's get even with some lasers!' he shouted out, as a transformation started to take place. 'ChromaStone!'

The alien hero's body glowed white hot for a moment – long enough to burn away the steel webs. The factory shook loudly as his feet slammed down against the floor, throwing up a cloud of choking dust.

As the dust began to clear, Spidermonkey saw a huge shape running towards him. It was

ChromaStone. He was charging forwards with his fists raised high up in the air. There was no time for Spidermonkey to move anywhere. He swallowed hard.

'Uh-oh,' he said. This was going to hurt.

Just before the impact, a brief burst of green light lit up the room. In ChromaStone's place stood Ben, his fists still raised but his confidence quickly fading. 'Uh-oh,' he muttered, realising that all of the transformations had exhausted the watch.

'Haha! Told you,' giggled Spidermonkey. 'You have drained your Omnitrix. Whereas mine will last . . .'

Spidermonkey quickly flashed back into human form, to demonstrate his own watch was still working perfectly.

'You see, I don't need an Omnitrix to destroy you, Ben Tennyson. I can do this all on my own,' Albedo cackled. He lunged forwards, swinging with a fierce punch. Ben did the same, throwing a punch of his own.

As the boys' fists passed each other they both cried out in shock. The Omnitrixes fizzed and sparked, pulling together like two powerful magnets. With a faint click they locked in place, trapping Ben and Albedo together.

'Aaaghh!' Ben shouted, as the sparks fell on to his skin.

'Get off me!' Albedo shouted.

'Do you seriously think I want to be attached to you, wise guy?' Ben asked.

Albedo yanked hard, trying to pull away. Ben heaved his arm in the opposite direction, but they only succeeded in knocking themselves off balance. Albedo hit the ground first, with Ben falling on top of him. The Omnitrixes began to spark and crackle even more.

'What's going on?' Ben demanded. 'Are you doing this?'

'No. Their proximity is creating a bio-energy feedback,' Albedo replied, before one of the sparks hit him. A sudden change swept over the boy. His brown hair became as white as snow, while his green jacket turned the colour of dark, blood red.

'No confusing those two now,' muttered Kevin, who was still struggling with Gwen to be free of the foam.

The change caught Ben by surprise, allowing Albedo to flip him over on to his back. Now Albedo was pinning Ben to the floor.

'You have damaged this form,' Albedo snarled. 'You will pay.'

But Ben wasn't beaten yet. Twisting his body, he managed to turn Albedo around and wrap an arm around his neck. 'Tell me how to get these apart.'

'Perhaps if one of us could manage to die.'

'Don't tempt me,' Ben growled.

Kevin groaned. Although Ben had Albedo in a choke-hold, he was still pinned to the wall. 'Great. Now we're all trapped.'

'Come on,' Gwen urged, firing up her eye beams. 'One more.'

Flexing his muscles, Kevin pushed against the foam as Gwen hit it with an energy blast.

With a loud crack the hardened foam split open!

They rushed along the corridor just as Ben and Albedo struggled back to their feet, still fighting. A shower of green sparks exploded from inside the joined Omnitrixes. Then, to Ben's surprise, the watches separated all on their own. He looked up at Albedo and immediately saw the panic in the boy's eyes.

'He's here,' Albedo whispered.

'Who's here?'

'Azmuth.'

'You bet he is!' said a tiny alien, teleporting in. He craned his neck to look up at the humans. 'Azmuth of the Galvan, the true genius behind the Omnitrix.' He turned his gaze on Ben. 'You've overloaded the thing so badly I could sense it half a galaxy away. Those non-stop transformations are gonna break it.'

'I was just – '

'Save it. I know. Albedo, my former assistant, built an inferior copy.' He glared at

Albedo. 'I warned you that there could only be one Omnitrix. You ignored me.'

'Someone's in trouble,' said Kevin, quietly.

'I will not trust the universe's fate to an unworthy human such as Ben Tennyson,' Albedo snapped. 'If my Omnitrix cannot function, then I will have his.'

'I told you, the Omnitrix is beyond you. You could have doomed us all.'

'So the universe really was at stake?' asked Ben, shocked.

'If you'd lost the Omnitrix, yes. Albedo

only wanted it to restore his original form.'

'This human body is simply unbearable,' Albedo explained.

'I get that,' Kevin nodded. 'And the face is even worse.'

'Albedo, through your arrogant act of rebellion, you have proven yourself a lesser being,' said Azmuth. Leaping up, he removed the dial of Albedo's Omnitrix. 'You shall remain as you are, in a prison of your own making.'

'No! You can't!'

Azmuth nodded. 'I have.'

A flickering light surrounded Albedo and he began to teleport away. 'I hate you!' he screamed, before he vanished completely.

'He won't bother you again,' said Azmuth.

'I still have a few questions,' said Ben. 'Like, what's the watch really for? And how many aliens can I – ?'

'Look, kid. You alone have made the Omnitrix a force for good, in ways I'd never conceived. It's better to allow you to create your own way of using it.' He hopped up on to Ben's hand. 'For all my concerns, you're the only being worthy to wear it. And I'm not the only one who thinks so.'

'Who else?'

Azmuth smirked. 'It's a surprise.'

'Now you're just teasing,' said Kevin.

A shimmering light began to surround Azmuth and he began to fade. 'There are difficult times ahead,' he said. 'Be ready.'

And with that, the three heroes were alone in the empty factory. Ben wasn't sure he liked the sound of Azmuth's last words, but right now he had bigger things to worry about. He had a physics test in just a few hours – a test he had barely done any studying for.

Azmuth's warning didn't matter, he decided. If he could pass the physics test then everything would be fine. After all, if he could get through that, he could get through anything.